THE *Princess* IN **BLACK**
and the *SCIENCE FAIR SCARE*

THE *Princess* IN BLACK

and the *SCIENCE FAIR SCARE*

Shannon Hale & Dean Hale

illustrated by
LeUyen Pham

CANDLEWICK PRESS

Text copyright © 2018 by Shannon and Dean Hale
Illustrations copyright © 2018 by LeUyen Pham

First edition 2018

Library of Congress Catalog Card Number pending
ISBN 978-0-7636-8827-1

18 19 20 21 22 23 LEO 10 9 8 7 6 5 4 3 2 1

Printed in Heshan, Guangdong, China

This book was typeset in LTC Kennerley Pro.
The illustrations were done in watercolor and ink.

Candlewick Press
99 Dover Street
Somerville, Massachusetts 02144

visit us at www.candlewick.com

For all the teachers who help kids love science
S. H. and D. H.

To Vivienne, Roen, Sloane, and Hunter,
future scientists of the world
L. P.

Chapter 1

Today was the Interkingdom Science Fair. Princess Magnolia had never been part of a science fair before. She was excited! Also nervous. Feeling excited and nervous at the same time made her want to wiggle.

She grabbed her science-fair project, a poster that showed how seeds grow into plants.

She did not grab her monster-alarm ring. The Goat Avenger was watching the goat pasture today. He'd stop any monsters that attacked while she was gone. She was all set for a monster-free day!

Princess Magnolia walked to the train station.

The train was crowded.

A man squished her on one side.

A woman squashed her on the other.

In the middle, Princess Magnolia held her poster.

She was excited to share it at the fair. And she was nervous it wouldn't be good enough. But first, she had to keep the poster from getting squashed. Or squished.

Chapter 2

The Interkingdom Science Fair was crowded. Princess Magnolia worried that she wouldn't fit in. She squeezed between the tables. She scrunched between the people.

At last she found her friends.

"Hello, Princess Honeysuckle!" said Princess Magnolia. "Your mole habitat is amazing."

"Thank you," said Princess Honeysuckle. "Moles are my second favorite animal. After wolves."

"I like unicorns best," said Princess Magnolia. "My second favorite used to be bunnies. But now it's cats."

"I like dragons best," said Princess Snapdragon. "Also hedgehogs."

Princess Snapdragon was pouring hot water into a bottle. When she placed an egg on top of the bottle, the egg got sucked right in!

"That's amazing, Princess Snap-dragon!" said Princess Magnolia. "I don't know how you got an egg to fit through the opening of that bottle."

"I used a trick with air pressure," said Princess Snapdragon.

"Hello, Princess Sneezewort!" said Princess Magnolia. "Your blanket fort is . . . so tall!"

"I used a lot of blankets," said Princess Sneezewort. "And twine."

"I'm amazed it doesn't tip over."

"Yes, I worked hard to distribute the weight evenly."

"Wow, Princess Orchid," said Princess Magnolia. "Your project looks amazing!"

"It's a seesaw that can lift buckets," said Princess Orchid. "I call it the Bucket Boosting Teeter-Totter!"

"There are so many good projects," said Princess Honeysuckle. "I wonder who will win first prize."

Princess Magnolia hugged her poster. It felt small and silly next to the mole habitat. And the egg in a bottle. And the blanket fort. And the bucket lifter.

And Tommy Wigtower's talking volcano.

Wait, what?

Chapter 3

Excuse me," said Princess Magnolia, "did your volcano just talk?"

"Uh . . . no," said Tommy Wigtower.

"EAT," said the volcano.

"I think your volcano just talked," said Princess Magnolia.

"No, it didn't," said Tommy Wigtower.

"EAAAAT," said the volcano.

"But I'm quite certain—" said Princess Magnolia.

"It's not supposed to talk!" said Tommy. "It's supposed to erupt! I should have tried it at home first."

"Did you add baking soda?" asked Princess Honeysuckle.

"Yes," said Tommy.

"Did you add vinegar?" asked Princess Snapdragon.

"YES," said the volcano.

"But it still didn't erupt!" said Tommy. "So I added . . . some monster fur."

"MMM," said the volcano.

Or rather, said the goo inside the volcano.

The goo growled. And it grew. It growled and grew. Now it was taking up all the space inside the volcano.

"Hey, get out of my science project!" said Tommy.

"NO!" said the goo.

Tommy tried to pull it out. It stuck like the stickiest gum.

"Oh, dear," said Princess Magnolia. "Tommy hasn't made a talking volcano for his science project. Tommy's science project has made a monster."

Chapter 4

It's a monster!" somebody screamed.

"I'll go get help," said Princess Magnolia.

She squeezed through the crowd. She scrunched under a table.

When she came out the other side, she was no longer Princess Magnolia. She was the Princess in Black!

She made sure her mask was on tight. After all, no one knew that prim and perfect Princess Magnolia was secretly the Princess in Black.

"I'm here to help!" said the Princess in Black.

"So am I!" said another masked hero.

The hero jumped free of the blanket fort. She tripped on a blanket. But she hopped back up again.

"Good to see you, Princess in Blankets," said the Princess in Black. "This science fair needs heroes."

"Yes, I heard a monster took over Tommy Wigtower's project," said the Princess in Blankets. "And . . . uh, I happened to be nearby."

"Get out of my volcano!" Tommy yelled. From a safe spot. Behind a table.

"NO," said the goo monster.

It growled. It grew. It growled and grew.

"The volcano can't erupt when you're in there," said the Princess in Black.

"Also, you're squished," said the Princess in Blankets. "Find a bigger home."

"NO!" said the goo monster.

Just then, the pressure from the baking soda and vinegar did erupt. It erupted the monster right out.

Everybody screamed.

"EAT SCIENCE FAIR!" said the goo monster.

"You may NOT eat the science fair!" said the Princess in Black.

The goo monster tried anyway. But it only ate one thing. Princess Magnolia's poster.

"That's it!" said the Princess in Black.

So the goo monster and the Princess in Black waged battle.

VOLCANO RUMBLE!

BUCKET BASH!

TWINKLE TWINKLE LITTLE SMASH!

The goo monster did not go
back in the volcano.

Chapter 5

The goo monster poured itself into Princess Snapdragon's bottle instead.

"Behave, beast!" said the Princess in Black. "That is Princess Snapdragon's bottle."

"HOME NOW," said the goo monster.

Princess Snapdragon tried to pull the monster out. But it stuck like the stickiest glue.

"That's not your home," said Princess Snapdragon. "You don't fit in there!"

The goo monster had grown so big that it popped out of the bottle. And dived into the mole habitat.

"HOME NOW," said the goo monster.

"That's not your home," said Princess Honeysuckle. "That's the moles' home."

The moles and the goo monster couldn't all fit in there.

The moles felt jammed. The moles felt crammed. The moles bit the goo monster. It yelped. It leaped out of the mole habitat.

And dropped into Princess Orchid's bucket.

"HOME NOW," said the goo monster.

"But I need that bucket for my project," said Princess Orchid.

"And a bucket isn't a very good place to live," said Princess Snapdragon.

"Besides," said Princess Honeysuckle, "you don't fit."

"FIT," said the goo monster. "FIT IN."

"Fit in? Noseholes and elephants," said the Princess in Blankets. "I've got an idea."

"I know what you're thinking," said the Princess in Black. "Let's go."

The Princess in Blankets and the Princess in Black picked up the bucket. They ran toward the train station.

Three princesses looked at one another. And then three princesses followed.

Chapter 6

The train was crowded. Princess Honeysuckle was squished. Princess Snapdragon was squashed. Someone stepped on Princess Orchid's toes.

"HOME NOW," said the goo monster.

"Not yet," said the Princess in Black.
"There's not enough room here."

"It's a monster!" said someone on
the train.

The people on one side jammed together. The people on the other side crammed together. Suddenly there was plenty of room for the girls and the monster.

"HOME NOW?" asked the goo monster.

"No!" said the people on the train.

The goo monster sighed.

At last the train arrived at Princess Magnolia's kingdom.

The two heroes balanced the bucket on their shoulders. They carried the monster off the train. The people on the train sighed. Then the train sighed. It shuddered. And it rolled away.

The goo monster pointed a blobby hand at Princess Magnolia's castle.

"HOME?" it said.

"No, not there," said the Princess in Black. "Definitely not there."

The goo monster started to climb out of the bucket.

"Stay!" said the Princess in Blankets. "We're almost to your new home."

"We'd better hurry!" said the Princess in Black.

But the bucket was heavy. It was so heavy that the heroes couldn't carry it and run.

"I can help," said Princess Snapdragon.

She squished in with the heroes. But there wasn't room for three girls to hold one bucket.

"I wish we had Princess Orchid's Bucket Boosting Teeter-Totter," said Princess Snapdragon.

"Or some way to make carrying this bucket easier," said Princess Orchid.

"If only we could all share the weight," said Princess Honeysuckle.

"I have an idea!" said Princess Orchid. "Princess in Blankets, do you have extra blankets?"

"Great idea!" said Princess Honeysuckle. "If we put the blanket under the bucket —"

"And we each hold on to the edge of
the blanket —" said Princess Orchid.

"We can distribute the weight evenly!" said the Princess in Blankets.

Some say that princesses don't run. But these five did. They ran very fast. And carried a monster between them.

Chapter 7

The goo monster was hungry.

All it had eaten today was one small science-fair poster.

One small science-fair poster was not enough food for a growing goo monster.

Every time it tried to eat something, a princess shouted at it. And every time it tried to find a home, a princess shouted at it.

Princesses were very confusing. And shouty.

Now five princesses were giving it a ride in a bucket. The goo monster enjoyed bucket rides. But it was still hungry.

The goo monster leaned over. It tried to nibble on some princess head fur.

"Behave, beast!" said the Princess in Black.

The goo monster did not know how to behave. It did know how to eat fur. So it tried again.

"You may not eat my hair," said the Princess in Black.

The goo monster sighed. It did not fit in with volcanoes. It did not fit in with bottles, moles, or buckets. It especially did not fit in with princesses.

Where could a goo monster fit in?

Chapter 8

Back in the goat pasture, a purple monster had come out of the hole. The hole that led to Monster Land.

"EAT GOATS," said the purple monster.

"Not today!" said the Goat Avenger.

The Goat Avenger enjoyed saying "Not today!"

Also "Not on my watch!"

And "Back, monsters! Back to your infernal pit!"

Shouting battle cries was the best

part of being a monster-battling hero. Sometimes the battle cries scared the monsters away. But mostly the monsters just wanted to eat goats.

The Goat Avenger would not let monsters eat the goats! So the purple monster and the Goat Avenger prepared to wage battle.

Waging battle was the second-best part of being a hero.

Just then the Princess in Black came running into the goat pasture! With the Princess in Blankets! Also three other princesses!

It was a whole princess herd.

"EAT GOATS—" the purple monster started to say. But then it noticed something. A goo monster in a bucket. It smiled. "NEW FRIEND?"

The goo monster slid out of the bucket. It squished and squashed over to the hole. It looked down.

"FIT IN?" it said.

The purple monster nodded. "FIT IN! EAT MONSTER FUR! EAT TOENAIL CLIPPINGS! BIG FUN MONSTER LAND!"

"NEW HOME," said the goo monster.

And they both dropped into the hole.

Chapter 9

The five princesses plopped down on the grass. They all sighed.

"What just happened?" asked the Goat Avenger.

"We ran," said the Princess in Black.

"All the way from the train station," said the Princess in Blankets.

"Carrying a heavy monster," said Princess Honeysuckle.

"In a bucket!" said Princess Orchid.

"I'm tired," said Princess Snapdragon.

"I'm pooped," said Princess Orchid.

"That was . . . FUN!" said Princess Honeysuckle.

The princesses laughed.

"But I was about to wage battle," said the Goat Avenger. "And then my monster left."

"I'm sorry," said the Princess in Black. "Waging battle is fun."

"It's my favorite part of being a hero," said the Princess in Blankets.

"Mine too," said the Goat Avenger. "After the battle cries."

The heroes said, "Behave, beast!"

And "Not today!"

And "Back to your infernal pit!"

The three heroes laughed.

The three princesses sighed.

"I wish I were a hero," said Princess Honeysuckle.

"Me too," said Princess Orchid.

"But you are!" said the Princess in Black. "You were so strong with the bucket. And brave with the monster. And you helped it find a home."

Chapter 10

Back at the science fair, Princess Honeysuckle really, really wanted to win first prize. But she didn't.

Princess Orchid got first prize. Princess Honeysuckle cheered. Everyone cheered. Princess Magnolia cheered the loudest of all.

"Are you okay?" asked Princess Honeysuckle. "It's not fair. A monster ate your project."

"I'm happy Princess Orchid won," said Princess Magnolia. "And next year,

I'm going to work harder. Next year, I'm going to do something amazing."

Princess Honeysuckle smiled. She would like to work harder too. She would like to do something amazing.

Amazing, like making a Bucket Boosting Teeter-Totter.

Amazing, like battling a monster.

She looked at Princess Orchid. Princess Orchid looked at Princess Snapdragon. Princess Snapdragon looked at Princess Honeysuckle. At that moment, they were all thinking the exact same thing.

The Princess in Black was right.
They already were heroes. They just
needed disguises. And secret names.